To precious girls everywhere—
may you always shine with respect—
a gift of love that lights your
world in everything you do.

The Best Gift of All

By Cindy Kenney
Illustrated by the Precious Moments Creative Studio

Library of Congress Control Number: 2009924516

Kenney, Cindy, *The Best Gift of All*/Cindy Kenney for Precious Moments, Inc.
Precious Moments # 990044 (Tradepaper)
                 # 990043 (Hardcover)

ISBN 978-0-9817159-6-4 (Tradepaper)
ISBN 978-0-9817159-7-1 (Hardcover)

Printed in China

Table of Contents

CHAPTER ONE

Birthday Wishes

I could see the smoke from the candles on Avery's birthday cake tickle her nose. She held her breath and looked at her friends. We were all anxiously waiting for her to blow them out.

"Come on, Avery," I laughed. "I'm hungry!"

"I have to make my wish first," Avery said.

I wondered if birthday wishes come true. I could not remember many of the wishes I had made, but I did remember the last one. My dad told us we were moving to Shine, Wisconsin, where he was going to work as the new director of Camp SonShine on Lake Lightning.

We all looked forward to living near my Aunt Ella, who lives in Shine where she owns a craft store. My mom was happy she would get to live by her sister. My sister, Anna, was excited, because she dreamed of going to the university in Madison someday. I was sad to be leaving my friends.

When I made my birthday wish, I hoped for wonderful, new friends. As I looked around the room at all the girls, I knew that some birthday wishes really do come true.

Avery closed her eyes as the rest of us watched and waited. We were all members of the Precious Girls Club, a group my mom and Aunt Ella helped me to start so I could make new friends. We have a ton of fun when we get together!

Avery opened her eyes, sucked in a big breath, and blew. All of her candles went out, and everyone stood up to clap, shout, and laugh.

"Who wants cake?" Mrs. Wilcox asked, and everyone's hand shot up in the air.

"What did you wish for?" Nicola asked.

"If I tell you, it won't come true!" she giggled.

Avery was super excited about getting to wear nail polish and have her ears pierced. Her mom promised she could do both for her party. Avery was way smart. I have never met anyone who knows so much. She even gets extra work to do in school, because she's ahead of the rest of us when it comes to almost anything, except for being creative.

Avery would rather do a puzzle or a math problem than paint or draw a picture. She jokes about her lack of creativity all the time.

•   •   •

"I want the first piece, after the birthday girl, of course," Becca said.

"You just want that little chocolate bar," Nicola accused.

"So? I called first dibs."

"That's not fair," someone else said.

"Girls! Everyone will get an equal treat," Mrs. Wilcox said.

As everybody waited for cake, I excused

myself to go to the rest room at the community center where we'd gathered. Once there I heard a door open and saw Avery through the crack in my own door. She washed her hands, stood in front of the mirror, twirled around and caused her pretty, pink dress to swirl in the air.

Earlier that day I told Avery how much I liked her new haircut and dress. But Avery said she does not like the way she looks.

"Katie, my mom fixes my hair and picks out my clothes. I'm horrible with a comb and brush, and I always match the wrong colors. I'm just not good at that stuff," she said.

"Everybody is good at something different," I told her. "And nobody is as smart as you are."

"Yes, but being smart isn't much fun," Avery argued.

"It can be!" I said.

"How do you figure?"

"You finish your work ten times faster than I do. That gives you more time to do cool stuff."

We both laughed.

I watched Avery admire herself in the mirror. She touched her newly pierced ears and fanned her fingers out to look at the sparkly polish on them. Then she spun around again for another big SWISH!

All of a sudden another door opened.

Avery jumped! She had no idea she was not alone.

CHAPTER TWO

Is it Just My Imagination?

"What are you doing?" Jenny McBride asked, nudging Avery aside to wash her hands.

"I thought I was alone," Avery said, looking embarrassed. "I didn't know you were in here. Do you like my new nails?"

Jenny dried her hands and grabbed Avery's hand and said, "Not bad, but the color is too light. I'll give you the name of my nail parlor. They're the best."

"That's okay. I think if I want my nails polished, I'll have to polish them myself."

"Whatever," Jenny sighed. "What do you think of my new outfit? Isn't it amazing? I found it just in time for your party. I'm the first person in school to own it. Cool, huh?"

"It's really nice, Jenny."

"Nice?" Jenny asked. "It's fabulous!"

"I think Avery's dress is the prettiest I've ever seen," I said, interrupting them to wash my hands. "Avery, I love your new earrings too. They glisten in the light."

"Thanks, Katie. I didn't know you were in here too."

Jenny had her hands on her hips and was about to say something when Mrs. Wilcox came in and said, "Hey girls, your ice cream is going to melt."

We followed her back to the party.

"So what did you wish for when you blew your candles out?" Jenny asked Avery.

"If I tell, it won't come true," she answered, holding firm to what she believed.

"Yeah, right. Good luck with that," Jenny said. "So what kind of presents did you ask for?"

Avery shrugged. "An MP3 and a renewal to *Business Week Junior* would be nice."

"You're kidding, right?" Jenny said, rolling her eyes.

"Time for presents!" Avery's mom said as we all gathered around. "Here, open this one."

"Wow, thanks, Mom!" Avery tore through the wrappings. "Oh, a craft kit," she said without excitement.

"Honey, you're always worried about not being creative. This will help you experiment with your imagination."

I couldn't tell if Avery was pleased or not. She was so polite and thoughtful. She smiled and thanked her mom.

"You'll love painting. It's so much fun!"

Nicola said. She leaned forward to show Avery some of the things she could paint after she opened her new paint set.

"Thanks, Nicola."

Avery opened a variety of creative kits and materials. By the time she was done, she had everything she needed to sketch, cross-stitch, paint, mold, glue, sew, and build and design programs on a computer. She even had gift certificates for art classes at Aunt Ella's craft shop.

"Wow, you guys! I have to learn how to be creative now," Avery laughed.

I looked at Bailey and Lidia. We shrugged and wondered if we had gone overboard trying to help.

As everyone got ready to go home, I walked over to thank Avery for the party.

"I sure had fun today," I said. "What do you think about all those craft presents? Are you disappointed or excited? Be honest."

"Maybe a little of both," she smiled.

"You can take them back and get something else," I offered.

"No, I don't want to. I really think it will be fun to give everything a try."

"Girls, can I get your attention before you leave?" Mrs. Wilcox called to us.

"Next week the Precious Girls Club will meet at Aunt Ella's Craft Store. You'll begin creating Christmas gifts for residents at the SonShine Nursing Home and sick children at the hospital during the holiday season. Any questions?"

There weren't.

"Hey, you can start using all your new stuff. Aren't you glad?" Kirina said as she left.

"Looks like I'll be busy," Avery agreed.

We walked outside together where I saw my dad sitting in the car waiting for me.

"You really do look pretty today, Avery," I said.

"Thanks, Katie."

She waved good-bye. I wondered if we had ruined her birthday or given her the best gifts ever.

CHAPTER THREE

Diamonds Are
a Girl's Best Friend

"How was the party?" my mom asked the minute I came through the door. She was cooking something in the kitchen with my Aunt Ella and Anna.

"It was fun!"

"Did Avery like getting the craft projects?"

"I'm not sure."

"Oh? And why do you say that?" Aunt Ella asked.

"She thinks she's crummy at stuff like that. Instead of helping her to get better, maybe we just gave her a bunch of stuff she hates to do."

"Oh dear, that would be too bad, wouldn't it?" Aunt Ella frowned. "What did she say about them?"

"She thanked everybody and said she'll give them a try. Avery is always very tagfull."

"*Tagfull*, honey?" Mom asked.

"You know, when you're real nice about what you say to somebody."

"Oh! You mean *tactful*," Mom laughed.

"Yes, tactful, that's what I meant. Avery's convinced she can't be creative," I added. "Plus, Jenny McBride can't ever be nice to anyone."

"What has Jenny done now?" Mom asked.

"She always has to be the star, the first to get everything, be best at everything, and have better stuff than anyone else," I complained.

"What does that have to do with Avery?"

"Jenny made Avery feel bad."

"Hmm, sounds to me like Jenny just needs to learn to have a bit more respect for others."

"What do you mean, Aunt Ella?"

"Well darlin', if those who brag on themselves would love and respect others, then they might see their neighbors in a different light."

"But how?"

"It's a bit like putting sunglasses on. Without them all you can see is the bright light shining on you. Put on your sunglasses and things are evened out so you can see all around you much better."

"But how . . ."

"Stay with me," Aunt Ella smiled. "When Jenny looks in the mirror, all she sees is a bright spotlight on her. If she showed respect to others by treating them with love, courtesy, and care, then she'd discover that others would show her oodles of love too."

"I get it. That's why kids don't get along with Jenny. She doesn't treat them with respect."

"I expect that's right," Aunt Ella winked. "As for Avery, God made everyone special in some way. We'll find a way to bring out her creativity."

"Okay girls," Mom said, taking cookies out of the oven. "Who wants to taste one of these?"

"I do!" we all said at once.

Later I walked into my bedroom and found Patches sound asleep on my bed. He opened one eye when I came in and went back to sleep.

Then a flash of sparkling colors splashed across my room. I knew Faith was waiting for me. She twirled around the room and zipped past several times before doing a final spin right in front of me.

"Ta da!" she laughed.

"Bravo!" I clapped. "Aren't you dizzy?"

"I don't think so," Faith answered. "But if I am, I like it."

Faith is my guardian angel and best friend, but there is one problem—no one else can see or hear her. She sprang to life one day when I was feeling down, and we have been close ever since.

I loved Faith when she was just a beautiful dancing figurine inside the musical snow globe my dad gave me. Now that we hang out together, I am thankful she is a part of my life.

Faith and I talk about everything. She is a big help when I get into a pickle and don't know what to do.

"I don't see why we have to be so nice to Jenny when she isn't nice to us," I argued with her.

Faith zoomed around my room with a splash of twinkly white. "Two wrongs don't make a right."

"I know, but all of Jenny's wrongs don't make a right either. Yet she keeps getting away with everything," I pouted.

Faith SWOOOOOSHED across the room so fast that it made Patches' fur ruffle in the wind.

"Ruff!" he barked, then went back to sleep.

"Sorry, fella," Faith said as she fluttered back over to scratch him gently behind his ear. "Have you ever wondered why Jenny acts the way she does?"

"No," I said honestly.

"Maybe Jenny is struggling with something very difficult in her life."

"Very *philipopsicle*, Faith," I groaned.

"Why'd you give Phil my popsicle?" she teased.

"Huh?"

"I think you meant to say that I'm being *philosophical*," she corrected.

"Oh yeah, that's it," I realized. "I still don't get it, Faith. When I'm in a crummy mood, I don't get away with being mean to other people."

"I didn't say that she should get away with it. I just said to think about *why* she might be doing it," Faith said. "It's all a matter of respect."

"Aunt Ella said something about that."

Faith smiled and zoomed across the room again. "I really like your Aunt Ella!"

"Me too."

Faith flew over and picked up my beautiful Precious Girls Club charm bracelet. "What a lovely bracelet! Look, this charm is especially sparkly."

"That's because it has a sequin in the middle that looks like a diamond," I told her.

"What's so special about a diamond?"

"They're pretty and they sparkle in the light. My mom says, 'Diamonds are a girl's best friend,' but I think she got that saying from TV."

We both laughed.

"Oh, diamonds are also very valuable," I added.

"Diamonds are a lot like people, sweetie."

"They are?"

"You said yourself that they are very valuable. Did you know that diamonds come in different colors?"

"No."

"Just like people, they come in all shapes, colors, and sizes. Diamonds are found far below the Earth, deep inside of rocks that must be dug up."

"I didn't know that. If you have to dig them out of rocks, how do they come out so beautiful?"

"It takes time to carefully uncover the diamond and then polish it to bring out that sparkling, pretty look. That's why they're a lot like people."

"I don't get it."

"Just like diamonds, it takes some digging, uncovering, and polishing to see how valuable someone is on the inside," Faith smiled.

"Do you think Jenny is valuable on the inside?"

"Just like a diamond, Jenny may take some uncovering and polishing before we can see just how wonderful she is."

"Wow, I never thought of that."

"Next time Jenny bothers you, remember that she may be covering up the special parts inside of her. Think about what you can do to help bring those beautiful parts out of her so she can start shining like a diamond."

I thought about what Faith said. It made sense. After all God made everyone different. Even I show my crabby side on the outside sometimes. That is usually when I get into trouble.

"Faith, I think I need to go to the hardware store."

"Why is that, Munchkin?"

"I need a big shovel. When it comes to Jenny McBride, I've got some super big digging to do!"

CHAPTER FOUR

Butterflies Are Free

"As you see there are many projects to work on. You'll have a chance to make several gifts," Aunt Ella explained to the Precious Girls Club. We had gathered at her craft store for our weekly meeting. "We'll meet here for the whole month, and when we're done, we'll deliver our cards and gifts to the nursing home and the hospital."

"I'd like to do the cross-stitch tissue box."

"Jenny, you're just saying that because you knew I wanted to do that one," Kirina grumbled.

"I'll make the bird feeder," Nicola said quickly.

"Girls, if you don't get your first choice now, I'm sure you will next time. We need a nice variety of gifts, so let's go into this with giving hearts."

As nice as Aunt Ella was, the craft store soon became a free-for-all. Each girl scrambled to get the project of her choice. If she didn't get first choice, she argued with the girl who did.

Suddenly a loud whistle pierced the room and brought everyone to a screeching halt.

"Ladies!" Aunt Ella scowled. "Go back and sit down this minute!"

"But I've already started working on this… okay, I'm going."

Aunt Ella meant business. "This is very disappointing. The Precious Girls Club is all about using the marvelous talents God gave each of you to do wonderful things. How can you do that if you don't begin by showing each other respect first?"

"We're sorry," one of the girls said.

"That's a start. It doesn't matter who goes first or who makes the most. We must have respect for each other's space and desires, just as we respect each other's talents. Let's try this again, okay?"

Aunt Ella is one of the most joyful people I know. She's funny, kind, and everyone loves her. *Everybody* in town calls her Aunt Ella, even though she's *my* aunt. Yet as nice as she is, we all know that you better not cross her. Who would want to? You'd be losing one of your best friends in the whole world.

The look Aunt Ella gave us said: *Don't cross me*. So we didn't. Everyone got up and showed each other respect as we found a project to do.

"Delightful," she said, as if nothing had ever happened. "Avery, darlin', I'm sorry I missed your party last Sunday."

"That's okay," Avery smiled. "It was mostly kid stuff anyway."

"Kid stuff is the best kind of stuff!" Aunt Ella giggled. "Anyway I've got a little gift for you."

I could tell it made Avery really happy.

"Go ahead, darlin', open it."

Avery ripped through the tiny, shiny package and opened the box. Inside was a beautiful,

delicate butterfly necklace.

"Ooooo! I love butterflies. Thank you!" she said and reached out to give Aunt Ella a little squeeze.

"You're welcome. I heard you're struggling with how to be creative," Aunt Ella said. "This will be a reminder that you should always feel free to be whoever God made you to be."

"Why a butterfly, Aunt Ella?" Avery asked.

"Butterflies start out in their little cocoons until they can break free and spread their wings," she explained. "You're still in your cocoon, waiting to discover all the beautiful ways God made you."

Avery was blushing, but she smiled.

"It matches your earrings," I said.

"There! Happy birthday!" Aunt Ella said, helping Avery put her necklace on. "Now let's take a look at what you're trying to paint."

"I can paint a landscape. It's easier than trying to draw people," Avery admitted.

"Good thinking," Aunt Ella said. "Sketch the scene. Let me know if you need any help."

"I will."

We were having a good time and many projects were done. I painted Christmas ornaments. Nicola built her bird feeder. Jenny created Christmas cards and worked on calligraphy. Becca made a purse. Lidia made sock puppets. Kirina did cross-stitch. Bailey created string art, but now was making Christmas cards on the computer.

"Okay, girls, finish up. It's almost time to go," Aunt Ella warned.

As Jenny passed by with a new calligraphy pen, she stopped to see Avery's painting.

"What?" Avery asked as Jenny scrunched her face up and stared.

"I'm trying to figure it out," Jenny smirked.

"It's a landscape," Avery replied as some of the other girls started to take interest too.

"A landscape of what?"

"Just a landscape," Avery frowned.

"What's with all *that* stuff?" Jenny asked, pointing to the easel.

"It's rain. My mom said to paint how I felt. I felt like I was painting with a cloud over me."

Jenny sighed. "Next time take some of that pink medicine for your tummy so it doesn't look like you urped all over your picture."

Jenny giggled along with several others.

"Jenny!" I said. "That's not nice."

"Oh, pleeease, Katie. Did you see how she drew that picture? It's so bad it's a wonder that Avery knows how to *draw* a breath!" she laughed.

This time Jenny got a rousing laugh from

most of the girls as Aunt Ella came from the back room. Everyone returned to work, but Aunt Ella could see what had happened. She came over and put her arm around Avery, who stared sadly at her picture.

"It's hopeless. I'm never going to be a painter," Avery said. She took a brush, dipped it in black, and swiped several large streaks of paint over her work.

"Maybe not," Aunt Ella said honestly, "but that's okay, you know. Give yourself time. No one becomes wonderful at anything overnight."

Avery nodded.

As for everyone else," Aunt Ella said before we could escape, "please remember to show each other respect. No one is good at everything. God is pleased with our work when we use *whatever* talents we have to care for others."

"Thanks again for the necklace," Avery said.

"Next week will be better," Aunt Ella winked.

Afterward I stared at Avery's ruined picture. Three strokes criss-crossed the canvas. I stared at it and frowned. Gulp! I sure hoped next week was better for Avery too.

CHAPTER FIVE

Riddle Me This

"Today you'll be working on a creative writing assignment," Miss Marla said, as she looked at the class. "Every student in our school has a chance to enter this year's writing contest. Any winners will move on to the state contest."

"Ooo! How cool!" Jenny said, obviously out to win another trophy.

The rest of the class met the challenge with a mixture of groans and curiosity.

"For those of you who would like to enter the contest, speak to me during recess. Now please take out some paper and let's begin."

As soon as the bell rang for recess, I ran over to Avery and asked her if she was going to enter the writing contest.

"I don't think so," she said. "I've got a lot to do and my mom expects me to help with the baby."

"Come on, Avery, your mom would be super proud of you for entering," I argued. "You are so smart. This is something you'd be really good at!"

"I don't know. The last thing I need is to give Jenny McBride something else to laugh about."

"Avery, don't pay any attention to her. Let's go find out about the contest."

Avery shrugged, "Maybe tomorrow." Then she took her turn jumping rope.

I walked over to Miss Marla, who was talking to some kids interested in the writing contest.

"Katie, you're interested in submitting a story for the contest?" she asked.

I laughed, "Oh no, not me! I'm trying to convince Avery to enter."

"That's an excellent idea, but there's no reason why both of you can't do it."

"You haven't read many of my stories," I said.

"I've read a few. I think you'll do just fine. Here," she said, handing me two entry forms.

"Thank you." I put the forms in my backpack.

"Katie Bennett, don't tell me *you're* entering the contest," Jenny said, watching my every move.

"What if I am?"

"Oh, go right ahead!" she giggled. "I'm not worried about entering against you."

I scrunched my nose and made a face at her, but then I felt dumb for doing it.

The bell rang and we all hurried back to class to work on our stories. Before we left for the day, Miss Marla gave us our weekly riddle.

"What can run but never walks, has a mouth but never talks, has a head but never weeps, has a bed but never sleeps?"

Everyone made silly guesses. Then we all scribbled the riddle down in our notebooks and headed for home. I hurried to catch up with Avery.

"Hey, Avery! What did you get on your math test?"

She turned and said, "One hundred and four."

"You got higher than a perfect score?"

"There were extra credit points, silly," she laughed. "What did you get?"

I sighed, "I'm crummy at math."

"I'll help you figure out what you did wrong, if you want."

"Really? That would be great, and I've got the perfect gift for you in return."

I pulled out an entry form for the writing contest. "Here you go."

Avery took the folded yellow sheet of paper and opened it up.

"Katie!" she groaned.

"Come on, Avery. Please? What have you got to lose? If you don't win, who's going to know?"

I could tell she was thinking about it.

"Besides, did you see who else is entering?"

She shook her head.

"Most of the kids *you* helped learn to write!"

We both laughed.

"Okay," she said. "I'll enter if you enter."

"Very funny," I said, but she meant it, and suddenly I heard myself saying I would.

We said good-bye at her corner. As I walked home alone, I realized I had just agreed to enter a writing contest. Me! I must be losing my mind.

CHAPTER SIX

The Written Word

I crumpled my paper and tossed it in the trash.

"She shoots and scores!" Faith said. "Good, you're smiling. That's better. You were frowning so hard I thought your face was going to stay that way."

"I can't believe what I've gotten myself into. I'm crummy at writing stories, and I'll never win this contest. What's the point in trying?"

"If you always felt that way, you'd still be drinking from baby bottles and getting diapers changed. Nobody's born being able to do much."

"No wonder life is so hard," I scowled.

"Well, the English language can be a little frustrating. I don't know why some of those rules were made," Faith said, zooming across the room.

"Which rules?" I asked curiously.

"Well, if vegetarians eat vegetables, what do humanitarians eat?" she giggled.

I laughed and said, "I never thought about that. What else?"

"There aren't any eggs in eggplant. There's no ham in hamburgers and not a single apple in pineapples."

"That's funny!"

"But true," she said, dancing about the room.

"Tell me more, Faith," I said, happy to be doing anything other than writing my story.

"Let me see," she said. "Reading and writing is hard, you see. There are so many rules from A to Z. Some make sense, but others, no way. Let's take a look at the rules we obey."

I knelt on my bed, bouncing up and down with excitement, anxious to hear more.

"When the *stars are out*, they're *visible*, but turn lights out—*invisible*! You *play* at a *recital* but *recite* when in a *play*. No matter how you look at things, be careful what you say.

"I can't remember *plague* or *plaque*, and who can spell *cul-de-sac*? Is it *bullet, bouquet, ballet*? How's your spelling? Hope it's okay! Take a look at *gruff* and *puff,* but then there's *sheriff* and *mischief*! I just want to yell "Enough!" But just wait, for I'm not *through*. I don't want you to be *blue*! Can you try to spell *adieu*? Or how about *boo, two, crew,* or *do*? Don't be fooled by words like *ache* and *break*, for if you do, oh goodness sake!

"Then there's *word, bird, nerd* or so I've *heard*! So many spellings it's *absurd*. Just compare a word like *wheel* right beside *appeal* and *heel*. Then take a look at *pea* or *brie*. But don't forget *TV* and *key*. I think you'll *agree* that it's quite a *potpourri*!

"Perhaps you think I'm clueless, but these words make me feel foolish. My advice is pay *attention* to your writing; did I *mention* that these words can be *confusing*? So be careful what you're *using*!"

Faith gave a little curtsy, then collapsed on my bed, and we both cracked up laughing.

"Yeah!" I applauded loudly. "That was super cool, Faith. Can you do it again?"

"You're not getting out of writing that easily."

"Bummer," I grumbled.

"Hey, you've got one thing going for you."

"Really? What's that?"

"At least it's not a math contest," she winked.

"Whew! You're right about that!"

CHAPTER SEVEN

Reuse-Reduce-ReSPECT

"Look! It came out just perfect," Becca said as she held up the wreath she made out of jingle bells.

"Well done," Aunt Ella said. "Be gentle with it until all of those jinglers have dried."

"I will."

"What are you going to make next?" Nicola asked.

"I think I will build a planter. My mom gave me an offshoot from a plant to start out with."

"That's a lovely idea," Aunt Ella said.

"Is there room for me at the wood station?"

"I'm afraid you'll have to wait until next week. Everyone left quite a mess last week. If you remember our discussion on respect, I'd like to talk about that a bit and ask all of you to help me clean up when we're done. Don't forget to reuse and recycle the supplies and things that are left over!"

"Aunt Ella, I have a good idea," I said. "You know a lot about recycling. Why don't you teach us how to reuse, reduce, and recycle! We could make some of your cool projects using recycled materials."

"That's a fantastic idea, Katie, but I think we have our hands full this month. How about if we put that on the calendar for Earth Day?"

The girls were very anxious to hear more about the recycling projects, and everyone agreed to put it on the calendar for April.

"Take a few minutes and finish what you're working on. Then we'll clean up together."

No one wanted the fun to end—except Avery. She heaved a big sigh as she stared at the napkin holder she tried creating from craft sticks. As she reached up to move it from the table, it crumbled in her hand. Earlier she had attempted cross-stitch, but wound up stitching her project to the front of her shirt. She was ready to go home.

"Pssst, Avery, did you get the threads out of your shirt?" I asked.

"Yes, but it left some holes that I don't think will go away."

"Will you get into trouble?"

"No, my mom is busy with the new baby."

Jenny put her project away, and on her way back she stopped by Avery's station. She placed her hand on her hip and shook her head. "Looks like somebody had sewwwwww much fun today!"

She and several others giggled.

"Knock it off, Jenny," I said.

"I didn't say anything bad," Jenny whined. "I'm just checking to see if Avery is okay. I heard she was over here in *stitches,*" she giggled. Some of the other girls couldn't help but let a laugh escape too.

I pursed my lips together and glared at Jenny.

"See, Katie? What I said was *funny*! But then I couldn't have done it alone. I needed Avery's help to keep us all in stitches!"

"Okay girls, I need your help," Aunt Ella said. "Why is taking the time to help others an excellent way to show respect?"

"Because respect is all about caring for others," Nicola answered.

"Good answer!"

"I don't get it," Jenny said. "Why not hire someone? We have a maid to clean up at home."

"Why do you have a maid?" Aunt Ella asked.

"To *clean—the—house*," Jenny said, pronouncing each word slowly.

"You're forgetting that both your mom and dad work very hard. Out of respect for your family, your parents chose to use their hard earned money to hire someone to clean so they can spend time with you as a family."

Jenny scrunched up her face. "I never thought about it that way."

"Perhaps you should. Your parents work hard to hire that maid. And you must respect your maid who works hard to make life better for you."

Aunt Ella got all of us thinking about that one!

"Think about helping me clean up here. Or cleaning up after a meal at home, or cleaning your room, or helping a teacher at school. How does that make the person you are helping feel?"

"Good!" everyone agreed.

"Showing respect is treating others the way you would like to be treated," Aunt Ella said. "If you go through life doing that, you will be surrounded by others who care about you. It will lead to a much happier life."

Aunt Ella gave us all a lot to think about and we couldn't argue with what she said. It made sense! I glanced over at Jenny to see if she got the message too, but it was hard to tell.

Everyone pitched in to clean up, and Aunt Ella's craft shop looked spic and span in no time. The girls left excited about what project they would work on next. Unfortunately, Avery wondered which project she could work on that would cause the least amount of damage.

CHAPTER EIGHT

And the Winners Are . . .

Miss Marla marched our class to the gymnasium for the big assembly. Everyone was excited to hear if anyone had won the writing contest. I hoped that Avery's story won. Even though I let her read mine, she would not let me see hers.

I talked to all our friends and told them to yell and shout super loud if Avery won. Then Jenny McBride made me go around and tell all the girls to do the same for her when she *did* win.

The school band played some songs at the start of the assembly. Then the choir sang "Somewhere Over the Rainbow." As they sang I hoped Avery's dream was about to come true.

When they finished, Principal Arnold walked to the podium and started talking about the contest. He said he was pleased to announce that several stories from our school had won.

As he spoke, some boys came in late, talking and laughing. Principal Arnold was not happy.

"Excuse me, young man," Mr. Arnold said. "Would you mind telling me why you're late?"

The boy stood up and said, "No sir. It was a sign down the road that caused us to be late."

Mr. Arnold looked at him over the top of his glasses and said, "What does a sign have to do with that?"

"The sign said, 'School Crossing. Go Slow,'" he laughed.

The entire gymnasium burst into a roar of laughter, right along with the boy. Principal Arnold waited patiently until we stopped.

"I don't appreciate your joke or your being late. Not only are you being disrespectful to me, but you're also being disrespectful to every other student in this room. See me in my office after school."

"That's so rude," Jenny whispered to Kirina.

I wondered how Jenny could see how those boys were rude but not see it in herself? I didn't get it.

"As I announce the winners of the writing contest, I'd like you to come forward to receive your award certificate and stand beside me."

I crossed my fingers, hoping he'd call Avery.

"Our first three winners are Jeremy Peters, Eliza O'Hara, and Jenny McBride," he announced.

I couldn't believe that Jenny won. I crossed my arms in front of my chest and scowled. "Come on," I whispered, "please read Avery's name."

"The next three winners are Steven Pulowski, Linda Gomez, and Katie Bennett."

"Katie, you won!" somebody said.

I just blinked. Me? Did he really read *my* name? I must have misunderstood.

"Katie! Go down front!" Nicola nudged.

I finally snapped out of it. I won! Wow! The kids were clapping for me. I hopped down several bleachers and accepted my certificate. Then it dawned on me, he hadn't called Avery. I wasn't supposed to win the contest.

I looked up at Avery, still sitting in the bleachers. Our eyes locked, and she gave me a faint smile. This was a huge disaster!

CHAPTER NINE

I Want to Be in Pictures

After we received our certificates, the principal asked the kids to give us another round of applause, which they did. I saw my sister, Anna, clapping hard off to the side. I had to admit it was super cool to have everybody clapping for me. I couldn't wait to tell my mom, dad, and Faith.

"Congratulations to each of you," Principal Arnold said. "But before you sit down, I have one more student to recognize. I saved this name for last because we were so thrilled to read such an amazing story from a young student. The first place winner of the writing contest is Avery Wilcox!"

I jumped way up in the air and started cheering as loud as I could. Avery's face lit up as she bounced down the steps to join the rest of us.

"Good job, Avery," Mr. Arnold said. "What a great group of students representing our school in the contest. Each one of you is eligible to submit another story for the Wisconsin state writing contest. Shine has never had seven students selected for this honor. We are very proud of you."

The band played as everybody congratulated us. Miss Marla gave us big hugs.

"Way to go, girls! We'll celebrate all three winners later this week," Miss Marla said.

Avery and I could hardly stop giggling; we were so happy. I wasn't too excited about writing another story, but I got through it once, so I figured the second time might be a little easier.

After the assembly a reporter from the *Shine Daily News* was there to get our names and take our picture. We held our certificates in front of us as the reporter clicked off several shots.

Then they took Avery aside to get her photograph by herself.

"Why does *she* get to have a picture by herself?" Jenny whined. "We should each get one."

"Avery came in first place," I said. "I can't wait to read her story."

"I can," Jenny groaned. Then she mumbled all the way back to our classroom. She was not happy that Avery's award was better than hers.

Back in the room some of the kids gathered around Avery's desk and asked for her autograph.

"Okay, everybody, let's give our star some space," Miss Marla said. "Avery, when you're famous, we can say we knew you way back when."

Avery was beaming with pride. Jenny was fuming.

As we began our spelling lesson, I heard Bailey whisper to Jenny, "I hope you guys win the state contest too."

Jenny looked at Bailey and grinned. "You can count on my story being a winner," Jenny said, "but I wouldn't place any bets on Avery."

Why would Jenny say something like that? And why was she suddenly smiling? "Jenny McBride," I whispered to myself, "what are you up to now?"

CHAPTER TEN

This You Did for Me

"Mom!" I called as I came in the door after school. "Mom! Where are you?"

"What is it, honey?" she asked, quickly coming into the kitchen to greet me. "Is something wrong?"

"No. Something is right! I won, Mom, I won the writing contest!"

"Oh, honey. That's amazing. Congratulations!"

"Avery won first place. Can you believe it? I couldn't. You should have seen it, Mom." I was so excited to tell her all about it.

"I'm really proud of you, Katie. You worked hard on your story and it paid off. Was Anna there to see you get your award?"

"Yes! She cheered the loudest of all! Oh, she's staying after school to help her teacher."

"Thanks, honey. She told me last night.

Why don't you head upstairs and get a jump on your math homework? You've still got to work on bringing that grade up."

"I think I'll become a writer. Then I don't have to do any icky math."

"You'll be surprised how many different ways you'll need your math skills when you grow up."

"Huh?"

"If you don't know math, how will you manage all that money you'll make as a famous writer?"

We both laughed.

I ran upstairs and told Faith all about what happened. She was super happy for Avery and me. Actually, she was even pleased for Jenny too. *Whatever*, I thought.

"Katie," Anna called, barging into my room.

"Don't you knock?" I asked.

"Sorry, but I know something you'll want to hear."

"Really? Spill."

"Mrs. Stevenson had me hanging projects in the hall outside Principal Arnold's office when guess who got called in?"

"Beats me."

"Avery Wilcox!"

"Oh no! Did she get hurt? Is she okay?"

"Yes, yes. But she was in trouble."

I thought for a minute and frowned. "What do you mean? Avery never gets into trouble."

"Well she did this time, and she's in very big trouble too. She got caught taking someone's bracelet."

"That's impossible. Avery would never do anything like that. You're wrong."

"No, I'm not. She had a teacher's bracelet on her desk."

"How did it get there?"

"I guess she put it there when she took it. Somebody saw her and told Mr. Arnold. He said she's going to be disqualified from the writing contest."

"What? That's not fair!"

"She's lucky she's not kicked out of school."

When Anna left I was fuming.

"Are you finished?" Faith asked.

"I don't know," I groaned. "Faith, there's no way Avery took that bracelet. The only thing she wears is her Precious Girls Club charm bracelet. She loves it. I'm sure Jenny did this."

"And you know this because she had a funny look on her face? That's not exactly proof."

"Maybe not, but I'm sure of it, Faith. I'm going to tell Miss Marla in the morning."

"You can't accuse someone of something you aren't certain about."

"But I am!"

"Don't you remember our discussion about being respectful?"

"Of course."

"You have to show both Jenny and Avery respect by being honest."

"Oh Faith, if you could just see how mean Jenny can be sometimes," I pouted. "She doesn't deserve respect."

"Can I ask you a question, Munchkin?"

"Of course."

"Is this how you would treat God?"

"What? That doesn't make sense."

"Let me tell you a story. A lovely young girl went to heaven. When she got there she met God.

"'Kyra!' God said. 'So nice to see you.' God gave her a big hug. 'I haven't seen you in a while.'

"The little girl looked confused. She didn't understand. 'But, God, I never met you in person before today.'

"God looked at Kyra and said, 'Sure you did. Two years ago you were in the park with your dad. He was busy, but you saw a man sitting alone on a bench. You offered to share your lunch with him. He was hungry and you fed him.

"'Last summer, when it was so hot, you had a lemonade stand. There was a woman who didn't have any money, but you saw how terribly hot she was, and you gave her a big cup of lemonade to drink. She was very thankful.

"'Last winter a young man had nowhere to go, but you told your parents, who took him in and gave him clothes to wear so he could get a job.

"'Last Christmas you visited some older people in the hospital. They were lonely, but you and your friends sang to them. It made them feel better than any medicine,' God said."

"'Little Kyra, don't you see? Whatever you did for each of those people, you also did for me. Every time you showed your love to others, you also showed how much you loved me.'"

Now I understood what Faith was saying. "So when I show respect to others, it also shows how much I love and respect God?"

"Yes, Katie, it does. Of all the things you can give to others, showing your respect is the best gift of all."

CHAPTER ELEVEN

Sherlock Holmes on the Loose

The next day in school, everyone was talking about what Avery did. I still didn't believe it. I got there early and waited for her.

"What happened?" I asked.

"Beats me," Avery answered. "But I didn't do it, Katie, honest."

"I know you didn't!"

"You do?"

"Of course I do, silly."

She reached out and gave me a hug. I could tell that she'd been crying, but her face was filled with relief when she saw that I believed her.

"We'll find out who did this to you," I said. "We won't give up until we do."

"Are you going to dust for fingerprints, Sherlock?" Avery joked.

"At your service!"

All morning I asked kids if they had seen anything, but no one had. Whoever saw the theft was staying quiet. The teachers were keeping it secret too.

"Okay, everyone, I've got the answer to this week's riddle," Miss Marla said as we took our seats. "Just a few of you figured it out. Avery, would you share the answer with us, please?"

"What can run but never walks, has a mouth but never talks, has a head but never weeps, has a bed but never sleeps? It is a river," she announced.

We all clapped. A few kids slapped their foreheads, others said, "Oh yeah!" while some groaned. Jenny was once again ticked off, because Avery knew the answer and she didn't.

During lunch I told Avery she should still write her story. After all, we had a whole week before they were due. I was determined to figure this out.

After I finally cheered her up, we returned to our classroom, but things went from bad to worse.

"Avery, may I speak to you please?" Miss Marla said.

Avery obediently walked up to her desk.

I was hoping it was good news. Maybe they had discovered the real thief.

"Is it true that you tripped a first grader coming into the building from recess?"

"What? No ma'am!"

"I have a report from someone that you did. Avery, please be honest and not make things any worse."

Avery frowned and her eyes filled with tears.

"I'm really disappointed in you," Miss Marla said as a tear slipped down Avery's cheek.

Avery rushed to her desk, grabbed her backpack, and left. I glanced over at Jenny, who was sitting at her desk grinning from ear to ear. I did my best not to blame her, but it wasn't easy.

After school Faith and I decided to wait and walk Avery home, knowing she would be upset.

"Looking for someone?" Jenny asked, coming around the corner of the school.

"I'm just waiting for Avery."

"She went home. Suspended, I think."

"You're kidding."

"Nope. But that's good news for you and me!"

"What are you talking about?"

"With Avery out of the contest, there's a better chance we can win," Jenny said excitedly.

"Avery *didn't* do anything wrong!"

"Come on, Katie. Don't be a drama queen. We didn't know Avery like we thought we did."

"Jenny, we should all be standing by her right now. She needs our support."

"Our support? I was thinking we should ask her to stop coming to the Precious Girls Club. That type of behavior is not what we stand for."

"Arrrrrrrr!" I shrieked and turned to walk away. If I hadn't, I would have done something

that would *not* show respect for Jenny McBride.

"Easy does it, Munchkin," Faith said, trying to calm me down, but it was useless. I was so angry!

I walked back into my classroom. Miss Marla was sitting at her desk, grading papers.

"Katie? Is everything okay?" she asked.

"No, it's not. Miss Marla, I know Avery didn't take that bracelet or trip that little boy."

"You do? Then tell me what you know," she said, anxious to hear the truth.

"Well, I don't really *know* anything . . ."

Miss Marla gave me a *you know better* look and said, "Katie, you need to stay out of this."

"But Miss Marla, please listen. Avery would never take that bracelet. She doesn't even wear much jewelry."

"She just had her ears pierced," Miss Marla observed.

"I know she did, but she's not interested in that stuff."

"Well maybe she wanted a bracelet."

"She didn't! She wears a watch on her left wrist and her Precious Girls Club bracelet on her right. She loves it and doesn't wear anything else, because she's collecting more charms."

"Actually, I thought about that too," Miss Marla said.

"You did?" I smiled.

"Yes, I know she loves that bracelet. In fact, Mrs. Hazelton thought her bracelet was lost. She found the clasp to it right before the assembly."

"Why would Avery take a bracelet that was broken?" I asked.

Miss Marla had already thought of that.

"Then she's not in trouble anymore?" I asked.

"Well, there's still the incident with little Robert Olson this afternoon."

"I don't know who said she tripped him, but it was super crowded by the steps when we went in. Anyone could have tripped him, Miss Marla. Honest, I was in the middle of the crowd too."

"I can't imagine why anyone would lie about Avery."

I bit my tongue to keep myself from saying anything, but Miss Marla must have noticed.

"Katie? Do you know anyone who would do this to Avery?"

This was my chance. Not only was it a chance but an invitation. "No, ma'am, I guess not."

"Thank you for sticking up for Avery. You are a very good friend, but don't worry too much. We know what a good student Avery is."

"She's not in trouble?" I asked again.

"Let's just say she's under suspicion. Let us take care of it. We'll make sure it's handled fairly."

I nodded and thanked her for listening.

Jenny watched me as I came out of the building. I didn't feel like talking to her anymore, but I decided I would at least wave good-bye.

CHAPTER TWELVE

R-E-S-P-E-C-T

It was the last day to work on projects. We were all anxious to deliver them next week.

"My mom is always saying that her favorite gifts are the homemade kind," Becca said.

"My gram says the same thing," Lidia added.

"I love them," Aunt Ella winked.

Suddenly there was a loud CRASH! Several bowls of beads tipped to the floor, and hundreds of little tiny balls went rolling all over the store.

"Oops," Avery squeaked and looked up to see everyone staring at her as she tried to make jewelry, she called herself "Fumble Fingers." Apparently old Fumble Fingers was at it again.

"No reason to worry," Aunt Ella said, hurrying to get a broom.

Avery felt awful. I was starting to believe Avery didn't have a creative bone in her body.

Avery stood up and headed for the door. I followed, but she stopped me. "Thanks, Katie, but I want to be alone." Then she disappeared into the back room. I saw Aunt Ella walk over to her.

"I'm so frustrated!" Avery cried. "I know how to do lots of things, but I can't pick up a simple craft project and make something? I'm the most uncreative person in the world."

Aunt Ella laughed, "Avery, darlin', you're quite creative!"

Avery looked at her as if she was crazy.

"Have you forgotten you won first place in the big writing contest! Don't you think it took a lot of creativity to put a good story together?"

"I never thought about that," Avery shrugged.

"Here, work this big old lump of clay between your fingers. It's good for working out frustration. Remember, you're just as creative as everyone else. Your gifts just come out in a different way."

Avery sighed and took the clay. She sat down at the table and squished it between her fingers.

The rest of us grabbed a broom and swept up the hundreds of little beads that were still rolling everywhere around the store.

"Guess what, everybody!" Jenny said, bursting through the front door as it jingled.

"What?" several girls asked together.

"I won first place at my piano recital! Even I didn't think I would win this time around. But I did it! Isn't it just the best news ever?"

Several girls congratulated her. Aunt Ella gave her a big hug. I noticed Avery listen as Jenny described her experience. I could only imagine that Jenny's win made her feel worse.

When Avery walked over to Jenny, I didn't know what she was going to do. "Congratulations! That's great news, Jenny," Avery said and reached out to give her a hug.

Jenny was startled and looked as if her chin would hit the floor.

"I didn't think you'd feel . . ." Jenny started.

Avery waited for her to finish.

"I've been teasing you a bit lately. I'm glad you didn't take it personally," Jenny said.

"No, I'm really happy for you, Jenny."

Jenny didn't know what to say. For her that was very unusual.

"Ummm . . . thanks, Avery. I'm sorry you got blamed for stealing at school," Jenny said.

"Well, it's not like *you* did anything. I just appreciate your believing in me," Avery said.

"Ummm . . . sure. Yeah, I do."

We finished cleaning up the store and left, anxious to deliver the gifts next week.

"You were amazing with Jenny," I told Avery as we walked home on a great, sunny day.

"It was the right thing to do," she said.

"You're right," I agreed. "You showed her a lot of respect."

"Besides, your Aunt Ella gave me a super duper frustration buster that helped," she said, showing me her big handful of clay. "I'll probably squish this clay until there's nothing left!"

I laughed.

"Plus, I've got good news. Miss Marla called and said Principal Arnold decided I'm innocent."

"Really? Yahoo!" I shouted. "I can't believe you didn't tell me before our meeting. Can you still enter the contest?"

"Yes," Avery smiled.

"I can't believe this! How cool."

"Your Aunt Ella told me things usually work out the way they're supposed to."

The only question remaining was if the real person setting Avery up would strike again.

CHAPTER THIRTEEN

True Confessions

Faith tagged along today because she knew the state winners of the writing contest were going to be announced during an assembly.

"Do you think anyone from our school won?" Kirina asked as we filed into the bleachers.

"Ah-hem!" Jenny said, clearing her throat. "If you girls had read my story, you wouldn't be asking that question."

"Oh, well, that's terrific then," Lidia said.

Avery and I grabbed each other's hands. We both hoped the other would win.

"I heard it's really hard to even get an honorable mention, you guys," Nicola said. "The guy who won in my class is a terrific writer, and he's never gotten an award in the state contest."

I frowned and shrugged. I never dreamed I'd win the first time around. But Avery? I still hoped that she just might get an honorable mention.

"Okay, everyone, settle down please," Principal Arnold ordered. "This is the moment we've been waiting for. As you know we had some wonderful writers in this year's state writing contest, and I have great news. Out of the students that went to state, we have two winners this year!"

Everyone applauded. The cheerleaders gave a rousing cheer and pumped everyone up even more.

"Our first winner took fifth place in this year's contest."

There were several "oooo's" and "ahhh's."

"I am proud to announce that winner is Linda Gomez! Linda, come on down and get your award."

The students went wild. Her class was

screaming and hollering. Linda was a sixth grader who had never entered before. She walked down front and accepted her trophy.

"This next student has taken third place in this year's state contest," he began.

Another eruption of applause. I saw Jenny sit up straight and tall. She was ready to leap forward and claim her prize. My heart was already sinking.

"Please help me congratulate our third place winner, Avery Wilcox!"

Both Avery and I leaped up and screamed, then hugged each other. Avery walked forward to accept her trophy as cameras flashed and the band started to play. Even Avery's mom and step dad were there to surprise her. The crowd went crazy! Everybody was super pumped up about her award.

"I didn't even get an honorable mention?" Jenny hissed. "*She* wasn't even supposed to be allowed to enter."

I sort of felt bad for Jenny. She was way bummed.

"Maybe you'll win next year, Jenny," I said. "You went really far this year."

"But *she* was disqualified because of what she did!" Jenny grumbled again.

"No, Jenny. They reversed the decision. They figured out that Avery didn't do those things."

"Well of course she didn't do them," Jenny said, not thinking about what she said.

"Really?"

Jenny scowled and crossed her arms. "I mean she's very honest. She wouldn't do stuff like that."

"I couldn't agree more," I said. "Isn't it cool that she won? We should all be happy for Avery today. Look how pleased she was for you last week when you won your award. It's time to show her the same respect. Don't you think?"

Jenny got quiet and didn't say another word.

After school we all gathered around Avery again. She was still glowing from her success.

"Are you ready?" she asked as I stuffed my mittens in my backpack. It was warmer than usual.

"Sure," I said, and we turned to leave.

"Hey, wait up!" Jenny called from behind.

We turned around as she hustled to greet us.

"Avery," Jenny said, "I umm . . . just wanted to say congratulations."

Avery was very gracious. "Thanks, Jenny. That really means a lot to me."

I was surprised that Jenny congratulated her. Maybe Jenny was like a diamond that was just starting to shine.

"There's something else too," Jenny said. "You've shown everyone so much respect, even me, although I haven't exactly done the same for you."

"That's okay, Jenny. You're being super nice now."

"No. I have to tell you that . . . I . . . ah, I'm the one who put the bracelet on your desk and told the teacher that you tripped Robert Olson."

Avery's eyes grew as big as saucers. She was stunned by what Jenny did, and I was shocked that Jenny confessed. Part of me wanted to strangle her for doing that to Avery, but another part of me was proud of Jenny for owning up to it.

"I've already told Miss Marla and Mr.

Arnold," Jenny said. "I figured I'd better come clean. I have to stay at school because my parents are on their way over. I just wanted to show you the respect you deserve and tell you what happened. I won't blame you if you never speak to me again. I'm really sorry, Avery. Honest I am."

Jenny turned to go back into the school, but Avery stopped her and gave her a big hug. They both squeezed each other tight for a minute.

"I don't understand," Jenny said. "Why are you hugging me?"

"It took a lot of courage for you to confess something like that. I forgive you, and I'll never forget that you came clean for me."

Both girls smiled, but Jenny's didn't last. Her mom and dad were headed down the sidewalk, and they didn't look as if they were in a good mood.

"Are you going to be okay?" Avery asked as she watched Jenny's parents approach.

"Sure. I don't get into trouble very often," she said, "or at least I don't get caught," she added.

CHAPTER FOURTEEN

Fruit of the Spirit

On the way to the nursing home and the hospital, Jenny offered to share some of her crafts with Avery.

"I've got more than enough," she said.

Avery smiled and said, "No thanks. I finally found something that worked out pretty good for me."

"Really?" Jenny asked.

Avery reached into her box of goodies and showed all of us a beautiful clay vase. "I learned how to work with clay while I was getting rid of my frustrations!"

The SonShine Nursing Home residents and the Shine Community Hospital were thrilled to get our gifts. We had enough for everyone. We sang songs for the seniors and told jokes to the kids. They thanked us over and over again.

After we were finished, Aunt Ella took us back to her craft shop. "The reason I brought you here is because I want to present each of you with something that *I* made for *you*."

We all eagerly waited for whatever Aunt Ella was about to share with us. She gave each one of us a small container that she had decorated in a variety of ways.

"Inside you will find a gold crown," she said. "This charm is for your Precious Girls Club bracelet. It represents respect—something I think each one of you has learned a great deal about. I'm very proud of all of you!"

The little golden crowns were beautiful. We all "oooed" and "ahhhed" and thanked her for the charms and all her help in the past month.

Aunt Ella took the girls home, but I invited Avery to drop by the house. "I've got a little something for you."

"For me? I know it's not my birthday. I already had one of those," she laughed.

"You don't need to have a birthday to get one of these."

I handed her a pretty box and watched as she carefully lifted out a beautiful angel snow globe. Inside the angel danced around the snowy winter wonderland.

"She's incredible!" Avery cried.

"Her name is Kyra."

"Ooo, what a lovely name. Thank you so much. Wow! I love her."

"*Kyra* means 'respect,'" I told her. "I thought you might appreciate that."

Avery looked at me and smiled.

That night I told Mom, Dad, and Anna all about my wonderful day. I tried to describe some of the amazing gifts the Precious Girls Club made for the residents at the nursing home and patients at the hospital.

"Aunt Ella is rubbing off on you, kiddo," Daddy said, "but that's okay. She's a terrific lady—just like your mom."

After we settled down to say goodnight to one another, my mom finished the day by reading a poem she had written for us.

"I wanted to write something that included the Fruit of the Spirit," Mom said, "because the fruit of showing respect is the love, joy, and friendship shared with others. My prayer for you is that you'll always live with respect and have others treat you the same way."

You're filled with love and caring,
With goodness, joy, and peace.
My daughter, please have patience.
May your goodness never cease.
You have learned to show respect,
You're trusting and you're kind.
Your cheerful disposition
Is very hard to find.

Your love and faith and courage
Are always so sincere.
You're sweet and understanding—
A joy to spend time near.
You look to God in all you do
With faithfulness and more.
My precious little girl,
I love to watch your spirit soar!
My daughter, I'm so proud
Of who you are and what you'll be.
I wish for you God's blessings
For all eternity.

Up next for the
Precious Girls Club: Book #5

Nothing but the Truth

"Come on Bailey. It's your turn," Nicola said. "What did you bring?"

Bailey reached into her bag and pulled out a huge trophy!

I did a double take. This wasn't just any trophy—it was enormous!

"Wow!" everyone gasped.

"I won this last year on vacation," Bailey explained.

"Gosh, Bailey. I didn't know you could run that fast!" Kirina said.

"I trained last year because my family raced," Bailey said.

She was trying to avoid looking at me, and with good reason. She said she'd never won anything in her life, but then where did the huge trophy come from? I couldn't wait to talk to her about it.

Although Bailey was very shy about her trophy initially, she opened up more as the group gathered and "Ooooed" and "Ahhhhed." By the time she was done, she made herself sound like Rocky Balboa training for his big fight.

I tried to pull Bailey aside and ask her what was up, but she was good at avoiding me and was the first one gone as everyone left.

Why would Bailey make up a story like that? I sure did want to find out what was up with that trophy.

**Read more in Nothing but the Truth
in stores Fall 2009**

A Charmed
Life Is Precious

Make a beautiful bracelet that tells your story and shows how precious you truly are.

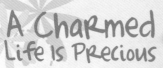

Respect Charm

We earned our Respect charm in this book! We gain Respect by giving it. Earn yours too!

Loving Charm

Helpful Charm

Kind Charm